Under Emily's Sky

This book is for Gutsie,
who helped me write it
just by being there.

THANK YOU, thank you to THE SLOGGERS, Linda Crosfield, Barbara Little, Marilyn McCombe, Thelma Rolinger, Helen Stevenson and Judy Wapp for their undying enthusiasm, support and helpful critiquing.

The setting of this novel is at a fictional beach and hillside. In reality, in September of 1936, Carr was camped on a sheep farm in Metchosin, which was then about ten miles out of Victoria. The 'elephant' was parked at the edge of a gravel pit, which gave Emily the wide views she loved for her paintings of the sky.

Lee wrenched herself from her mother's arms. "How do you know?" she yelled, clenching her fists. "How do you know we'll be better off without Dad? You have no idea what makes me happy." Tears came to her eyes and she turned away. "You don't know anything about me. Nothing. Why doesn't anyone ask me what *I* want?"

She ran from the living room, slamming the door behind her. As she passed her parents' bedroom she saw her dad standing with his back to her, packing a suitcase: shirts, pants, socks, model train engines, cowboy boots, everything thrown onto the big double bed. The section of wall where a framed picture of his favorite locomotive used to hang was now empty; only a faded patch of wall remained. Lee stormed down the hall to her own room, slamming this door even harder. Her paper kite fell off the wall and she kicked it under the bed in one swift, forceful motion.

Lee pulled the bottom drawer of her old dresser

open until it stuck. She yanked harder to get it past the grove and it slammed against her legs. "Arrrg!" she yelled, kicking it furiously. From under a sweater she picked up her journal and a battered cookie tin. She flung the lid across the room and grabbed a chewed-up pencil stub. She wrote:

My parents don't care how I feel about all this!!!!! They're too busy fighting to think about anyone but themselves. Mom tells Dad to leave and he stomps off for hours. When he comes home, it's always really late, sometimes in the middle of the night. He makes a huge scene, yelling and screaming, saying he wants to try and make things work. Sometimes he doesn't come back until the next night and it starts all over again. Why can't they just stop? Why doesn't he give up drinking? Why doesn't Mom make him quit??? Why, why, why?

Nobody in this house listens to me, especially Dad. I might as well be talking to his gin bottle. I told him to stop drinking. He promised he'd stay sober. Why does he lie?

She underlined *promised* so hard, the pencil tore the paper. Disgusted, she hurled it across the room.

Flinging herself on the bed, she banged her fists on her pillow. "You lied," she said loudly. Then she yelled, "You lied to me!" at the top of her lungs. She buried her face in her pillow, knowing he wasn't listening. He never listened. She knew he wouldn't quit drinking. Deep down, she also knew that Mom was right, that they *would* be better off without him. But to kick him out forever, for good?

As much as she hated Dad's behaviour, Lee wanted two parents. She'd give anything to have a family who would talk to her at dinner, take her on trips, and love each other like they did when she was younger.

There was a knock at the door.

"Go away!" she cried into her pillow.

After another knock she heard her father's voice. "I'm coming in to say goodbye."

Lee saw the door inch open slowly. She hid her face in the pillow.

He cleared his throat. "I'm sorry," he said. "Lately I...I haven't been much of a father." His usually gruff voice sounded funny, cracked. He cleared his throat again.

"Why didn't you just stop drinking?" Lee shouted into the pillow, gripping the edges of it with her nibbled fingernails.

"I just can't do it, Lee. And I can't live here any more," he said firmly. "I won't be coming back this time. She's pushed me to my limit." Lee heard the springs sigh as he sat down on the edge of the bed.

"What'd she do?" Lee looked at him sideways, her thick hair falling across most of her face.

"She phoned my boss." He stopped and slammed his hand on his thigh. "Never mind. It's nothing for you to worry about." He sat very still, looking at the floor, before he said, "I'm moving to Edmonton. I'm getting a job at a train station there. It'll be better than working at the bus depot. We'll still see each other. I'll take you on a vacation, on a real train." He patted her shoulder.

"That's not good enough." Lee sat up. "I want to live with *both* of you. Why can't you stay?" She looked into his eyes. They were the same blue as her own, but his weren't looking back at her. They seemed to look through her, as if she weren't even there.

"No. I can't. We've been through all this." He rubbed his unshaven chin. "You can come for a visit."

"When?" Lee scowled.

"Soon." His hands clenched into fists. They moved nervously against his jeans, tapping his thighs impatiently.

"You lied to me." Now Lee's fists were pummeling his chest, hitting him as hard as she could.

He held her wrists. "It's no use." He pushed Lee away so that her lanky body fell backward onto the bed. "I guess I can't do anything right." He jumped up and strode through the door, closing it behind him as he left.

His usual loud, angry footsteps thundered down the hall. The front door slammed. Suddenly the house was very quiet.

Lee wiped her face on the sheet and jumped up. Kicking the dresser, she turned her old tape deck on full blast. To the drum beat she kicked the bottom drawer of her dresser– *whack, whack, whack.* No one listened anyway, so why should she care?

Whack. Whack. Whack.

There was another knock at the door, loud, above the music.

"Go away!" Lee hollered. "Leave me alone."

She heard Mom's voice yelling something at her through the door, but she couldn't understand it. Her mother didn't come in.

Good. In the cookie tin Lee found another pencil.

It's <u>her</u> stupid fault!!!! She could have tried harder to make it work. Now I'm alone. I hate them both!! I hate this room! I hate this music! I hate this day! I hate <u>everything</u>!!!

Lee looked up at the wall at one of her favorite photographs hanging above the bed: a picture of she and her cousin Alex tubing at "The Slide" near their usual campsite. That's the picture she'd take with her if she left. If Dad packed his locomotive picture, he must be leaving for good. And he had said goodbye in a way that made it sound absolutely final. He had never done that before, ever.

I might as well run away too. Why stay in <u>this</u> place??? I'll go and live in the old, abandoned shacks in the hills. I'll tell Alex, he'll understand. I'll swear him to secrecy. He'll bring me scraps of food. I'll survive without them. I'm sure no one will even notice I'm gone!

She banged the covers of her journal shut. Maybe that was a stupid idea. Kicking the dresser harder, she turned up the music– loud, angry music– to block out everything, especially the word *goodbye*.

She lay on the bed, listening to her tape. When one side finished, it flipped automatically, and she tuned in and out, listening to song after song after song.

She stared at the ceiling, wondering if she'd ever see her father again. She'd hardly seen him these last few years anyway. He always came home late (even though his job at the depot ended at seven o'clock) and stayed in bed until after she left for school most mornings. On weekends or holidays, if he was around, he was cranky. Sometimes, when he worked on his latest model engine in the garage, he put the "Do Not Disturb" sign on the door and didn't even acknowledge she was home.

When she was younger he had taken her to the park, played ball and soccer with her, pushed her on the swings. That was before he started drinking so much. Since then it had been like Mom always said: "If he'd paid as much attention to his daughter as he did to his bottle, he'd have been a real father."

What difference did it make now? Mom was right; they'd be better off. He wouldn't spend all their money on liquor, they'd stop arguing, she'd know where she stood.

The gray spot on the ceiling, where water had once seeped through from the above apartment, shifted shapes before her eyes. Ugly shapes.

Her alarm clock read 7:12. Lee didn't feel like leaving now, but maybe later, after dark, she'd take off. She'd go to her friend Natasha's house and ask if she could spend the night there. She sighed. *I suppose I can stay here for now,* she thought, *but I'll definitely never talk to Mom again. Ever.*

Lee woke up at 6:14. She stretched and noticed she was still wearing her shorts and T-shirt. She was covered with a blanket and her shoes lay beside the bed. Minnie, her gray tabby, lay curled up beside her pillow, one paw outstretched. She started purring, but didn't move.

Mom must have come and tucked her in. Lee didn't remember waking up. Just as well. She'd be just like that with everyone from now on– asleep, deaf, silent.

She got up quietly, but stepped on the pencil stub. Swallowing her scream, she kicked the stub across the room.

With a longer pencil, she scribbled:

Another dreary day. I may move tonight. I won't even tell Alex. Maybe I'll live in the mountains–the bears and cougars should leave me alone. I'll eat berries. I'll make it on my own. They'll all be sorry!!!

She bit hard on the end of her pencil. Putting her journal in her pack and picking up her shoes, Lee walked to the front door. She'd leave early for school. Her stomach growled. She'd better take some food. Opening the fridge, she shoved aside the milk, cheese and bits of left-over chicken. Never mind her mother's rule about eating a healthy breakfast. Lee grabbed the bread and jam and headed for the counter.

As she rummaged in the drawer for a paper bag, her mother walked in, tying the belt of her faded cotton housecoat.

"You're up at the crack of dawn," she yawned.

Lee grabbed her sandwich and hurried to the front door. Why did her mother have to be up so early?

"Honey, you need to eat something." She pushed her uncombed auburn hair off her face. Lee noticed her puffy eyes. "I know you're angry at me, but you have to at least eat properly." Her mother sighed, trying to smile. Instead, her bottom lip trembled and her eyes welled with tears.

Turning her back to her mother, Lee bent over to put on her shoes. Slowly, she tied her laces. Why don't I just walk out? she thought. What would happen if *I* left too? If I yelled, "I'll never come back either!" and slammed the door?

Her mother stood in front of the door. Lee noticed her bare feet, the toenails she used to polish pink. Standing as tall as she could and facing her mother, she said, "What do you care?"

"Honey, I do care." Her mother's eyes reddened. She held her arms out. "This is really hard for me too, you know."

Lee backed away. She ran to the kitchen and banged the cupboard doors as she got her cereal. After slurping her orange juice, she purposely spilled part of her cereal on the table before eating a large spoonful. She left, flinging the front door shut behind her.

She slowed as she got closer to Natasha's house. She was too early. But what did she care about stupid Natasha anyway? She was going to spend the rest of her life being angry. Even at Natasha. Especially at Natasha, who had a nice dad and grandmother, even if they were terribly strict. At least Natasha had a family.

Lee ran past her friend's house, her pack bouncing against her back, and on to the school playground. The doors of the school were still locked, the grounds empty. It was Friday, the first week of school after the summer holidays. Lee's first week in grade seven.

Hurling her pack to the side, she sat on one of the swings. Her feet shuffled in the summer dust, then pushed hard off the ground. She started moving, back and forth, back and forth, back and forth, her long legs pumping the air as it rushed by her face.

Lee swung for what seemed like hours. Her legs grew tired and her head felt empty. When the first students got off an early bus, Lee jumped down, snatched up her pack and hurried to the far corner of the playground. She sat on the grass, her back against the metal fence, and took out her journal.

I'm never going back. Dad said he'd get me a dog. He promised to help me build a dog house. He said he'd paint my bedroom, let me pick the colours. He said I could even do it myself. He made so many promises!!! What a liar! He lied about meeting in Edmonton, too, I know he did. I hate it when people lie. Now I'll never see him again.

I won't go back! I wish I could live with Uncle Brooke. He doesn't lie, he doesn't drink, and he'd never walk out on Alex and me.

Lee looked around the playground. Some kids were playing soccer not far away. Twice someone called "hi." She didn't say anything. She needed a plan. She had to think.

Just as the bell rang, Natasha ran onto the playground. Lee jumped up and hurried to the far door.

The hall was crowded with kids yelling, locker doors banging and packs swinging back and forth.

Her pack! Lee walked back to the fence to pick up her pack and then sauntered back to the building. She was in no hurry to get to class. Natasha was nowhere in sight.

By the time Lee reached her locker, the hallway was almost empty. Her grade six teacher walked by.

"It's not like you to be late," she said.

Lee scowled, but didn't say anything. After throwing her pack into her locker, she banged the door shut and stomped to the classroom. She flung the door open (now that she was into slamming) and marched in.

Her new teacher, Ms. Candle, looked up from the attendance sheet. "You just made it," she said, erasing the *x*.

"So?" Lee sat down. She threw Natasha a dirty look, then focused on her empty desk top. Why was she acting like this? She didn't usually treat Natasha this way. They'd been best friends since grade three. Lee put her elbows on the desk and rested her head on her fists. She wasn't the sort of student who purposely caused problems. Sure, she'd gotten into trouble before, been angry or rude. Now she *wanted* to misbehave, to yell, to smash something. She was furious. She kicked the desk leg.

Ms. Candle asked everyone to take their binders out. "It's time for our writing assignment," she said cheerfully.

"Sure," Lee mumbled. "I'll write a story: *My dad, the drunk, takes all our money for booze....*" She scowled. I'm sure Ms. Candle would love a story about *that*.

Lee kept her elbows on her desk, her head on her fists.

"Lee, where's your paper and pen?" Ms. Candle walked along the row.

"I can't think of anything to write." Lee bent down

and found a pencil in the front of her desk. She took a crumpled piece of paper and smoothed it a little, looking up.

Ms. Candle took a pen from the desk and put it in front of her. "Yesterday you wrote a great story about the beach."

"That was yesterday," Lee muttered.

"Why not write about that beach again and what you found there. It sounded like an interesting place," Ms. Candle prompted.

"Why should I? I don't want to write a stupid story," she said loudly.

Ms. Candle frowned. "I'll ignore that this once, young lady," she said. "Get started." She turned sharply and walked down the row.

Lee saw Natasha looking at her with surprise, her big, brown eyes wide in her round face. She looked back angrily, then grabbed her pencil. Why write in pen? It would be all wrong anyway. Everything was all wrong. "I HATE my life," she wrote. She erased it. "My parents are splitting up." She erased that too. "It's no use," she wrote before crumpling the paper into a ball and stuffing it back into her desk.

She sat, her head on her fists, until Ms. Candle came by again. Lee told her to leave her alone.

Ms. Candle asked Lee to go out to the hallway for a talk.

"What's the matter?" The teacher ran her hands through her short, dark hair. Her olive-brown face wrinkled into a question mark.

"Nothing." Lee, looking at the floor, slipped her hands into her pockets.

"You don't usually act like this. Did something happen this morning?"

Lee didn't answer. She stuffed her hands deeper into her pockets.

"Do you want to talk?" Ms. Candle tried again.

"No!" Lee wanted to kick the wall, but at the same time she felt tired, empty.

She started pulling her hands out of her pockets. She *did* want to talk. She wanted to ask why these things happened, what she could have done to make things different. But then she remembered Mom's words, "It's best not to talk about it too much with others. They may not understand."

Lee pushed her hands deeper into her pockets and looked at the floor.

"You'd better wait here," Ms. Candle said. She walked to the office, her shoes squeaking on the linoleum.

"I phoned your mother," she said when she returned. "I'm sorry to hear your dad left. If you need to talk, I want to listen." After a short silence she said, "Just do the best you can today."

Lee didn't say anything.

Ms. Candle told her to go back to her desk. Lee sat there, doing nothing, thinking nothing until the recess bell rang.

Lee saw Natasha walking over before she'd reached the classroom door.

"I'm sorry. I waited for you as long as I could," Natasha said. "I was almost late myself. Where were you this morning?"

"Nowhere." Lee took her lunch from her locker. She ate the jam sandwich in a few hungry bites and kicked the locker shut, hard.

"What happened with Ms. Candle in the hallway?" Natasha asked before biting a piece of her banana.

"Nothing." Lee walked outside, her hands in her pockets. She didn't want to talk to anyone.

Natasha followed. "What did I do?"

"Nothing." Lee sauntered on.

"Bad day?" Natasha asked.

Lee only shrugged her shoulders and started walking away across the playground.

Natasha walked beside her for a bit. "What's bugging you anyway?" she asked again. When there was no answer she said, "Fine. Don't talk. I'm going to play soccer." She headed off in the direction of the field, her strong legs taking big steps.

Lee wished her pockets were bigger; she wanted to push herself deep into them and disappear.

After recess the students worked on the math Ms. Candle had assigned. Lee usually didn't mind math. Today she hated those stupid numbers. Next they went to music, down the hall. Lee hated singing.

By lunch time she was hungry, but she had nothing left to eat. Natasha chewed her sandwich. Lee tried to smile. It felt funny, as if her skin was too tight, as if a smile no longer fit her face.

In Ms. Candle's class Friday afternoon was set aside for art. She taught sculpting, weaving and drawing, and the best art projects were put in the display case.

Today Ms. Candle showed slides of paintings by one of Canada's most famous artists, Emily Carr. She talked about each slide, commenting on the vivid colours, the realistic shapes of trees and the swirls in the sky. She pointed out the difference between a photo of a tree and the paintings. "They're so rich," she sighed. "Artists are often extremely poor, but their work gives us such wealth. That's certainly true of Carr."

She went on to explain that Emily Carr had lived in San Francisco for a few years to take painting lessons and had then gone to Europe for the same reason. Later, she travelled around B.C. so she could experience the feelings, the smells, sounds and movements of what she painted. She visited the northern part of Vancouver Island, the Skeena and Nass river areas and the Queen

Charlotte Islands, and painted in tiny Native villages, even though she got sick on the boats, even though the mosquitoes were horrible.

"These were not easy trips, certainly no luxury, but she loved the totem poles and the huge trees. She never married and didn't have children of her own, although she liked children and gave talks at a few schools in the area. But she was a loner and she put her feelings into her art and her animals rather than into people.

"We can see some of her work in museums. Her paintings are worth a fortune now, but copies of them, prints, like this one," she pointed to a poster on the wall, "are relatively cheap."

Ms. Candle asked the students to imitate Carr's style of painting, trying to use the brushes with the same energy they had seen in the Carr paintings.

"Feel it. Reach deep inside yourself." Ms. Candle moved her arms up and out from her stomach in a dramatic gesture.

Lee loved painting, she always had. The trees they were supposed to portray, the trees right outside the classroom window, swayed slightly in the wind. Lee swirled her brush to make branches.

"Yes, good motion." Ms. Candle smiled, lightly putting her hand on Lee's shoulder.

Before Lee knew it, the afternoon was over. She and Natasha walked home together, not talking much. The closer Natasha got to her house, the more she slowed down.

"My grandma's having a quilting party on Saturday afternoon." Natasha sighed as she walked up the steps. "I have to wear my best dress and serve cookies and tea." She made a face.

"We're going camping," Lee said, not envying her friend. Natasha always had to act "properly" around her grandmother.

When Lee got home, Minnie sat by the front door, meowing in protest.

"Poor kitty. Are you miserable too?"

Lee stroked the cat and fed her before turning the music on.

In her journal she wrote:

I could never live at Natasha's house. No way. It's the woods for me. I'll wait till tomorrow or Sunday. Then I'll split. Go up to the old sheds in the hills....

Mom would be home any minute. She worked until 3:30 as a secretary in the high school office. She didn't make a lot of money, but with Dad gone, he wouldn't be able to spend most of it. Mom could buy things without borrowing money from her brother all the time.

Maybe he would come camping with them tomorrow in his motorhome. Alex, her cousin, and Pat, Uncle Brooke's partner, could all head out for an overnight at the beach.

Even though they went to different schools, she and Alex spent a lot of time together, camping and hiking. Uncle Brooke and Pat loved to cook and invited Lee and her parents over for dinner often. Dad had never come along.

"Hi, how was school?" Mom bustled in, dumping her purse and two bags of groceries on the counter.

Lee grabbed a carrot, the only thing she was allowed to eat just before supper. Her mouth full, she mumbled, "Fine. We painted."

"Your teacher phoned earlier. Did the morning improve after that?" She handed Lee the food to put in the fridge.

"Yeah," Lee shrugged. "Can we invite Alex and Uncle Brooke to come camping?"

"They're coming later, Saturday afternoon. I phoned Brooke from work. We'll set up camp tomorrow morning." Mom smiled. She looked tired and her cheeks were pale.

"Are you glad Dad is gone?" Lee slammed the fridge door shut. She had a funny feeling in her chest, as if something was pressing hard against her ribs.

"Yes, honey. Your father should have left years ago. He wasn't the kind of Dad you deserve."

Lee shook her head. "He used to be all right before...." She wanted to hit something. Then the tight feeling loosened a little. "Why can't I talk to anyone?"

Mom's eyebrows shot up. "You can...."

"You said I couldn't," Lee interrupted loudly. Her

hands curled into fists.

"Of course you can!" Her mother stood right in front of her. "But not to just *anyone*. Talk to me. Or your uncle, or your teacher."

"To you? What difference would that make?" Lee took a step back.

"I know I couldn't make him do what you wanted, honey," she shook her head, looking drained, her shoulders sagging. "But some things we can only do for ourselves."

"I guess." Lee walked to her room. She didn't slam the door, but she did turn the music up.

The only things I can do are write and paint—I can't even paint at home any more. I wish I could create another world with just the swirl of a brush—browns, greens, blues. I wish Dad hadn't sold my paints and easel at his stupid garage sale. He didn't even ask me!!! He just sold everything while we were out camping with Uncle Brooke. I wish he was my dad. He likes my paintings and he probably likes Emily Carr's too. He's always buying new prints from the Group of Seven painters, maybe he even has an Emily Carr print. I'm going to look at his collection next time I visit. If I hint, maybe he'll buy me a print for my birthday next month. I want the one called "Forest Landscape." I wonder what Emily Carr is like...does she have a diary? (Would I ever like to read it!!)

The eagle screeched overhead and dipped temporarily before climbing higher into the trees.

"There it is." Lee put aside the tube of sun block and, barefooted, walked slowly in the direction of the cedar tree. The bird perched on a high branch, his head swiveling this way and that.

Alex squinted behind wire-rimmed glasses. "I see it. It's gonky."

Lee nodded. Alex always had a favorite word. His latest was "gonky." Lee didn't know what it meant, or if it was even a real word.

The eagle spread its powerful wings, soared up from the branch over the trees and disappeared out of sight.

Two recreational vehicles were parked side by side at the edge of the tall trees just above a stretch of beach on the west coast of Vancouver Island. Lee and her mother slept in an old Volkswagen van. Alex, Uncle

Brooke and Pat stayed in their big, new motorhome. They were the only ones on that stretch of beach. Not many people knew about the narrow dirt road leading to this spot.

Climbing rocks, hiking, swimming in the cove and canoeing kept everyone happy for days. A long smooth rock formed a slide that shot them into the water when the tide was in. This morning the tide wasn't far enough in yet, but Alex had already put the tubes by the rocks in anticipation.

Lee sat down on a big boulder. From here she could see the beginning of the trail that led to the old homestead on the forested hillside. The homestead, set in a clearing, had two old, tumble-down shacks made of logs and rough planks. The walls had partly collapsed. Branches and creepers grew through holes, open doorways and an empty window frame. Lee and Alex had taken the fifteen minute hike there many times. They had told each other ghost stories, climbed the old apple trees and had used the unripe fruit for target practice.

Lee wanted to go up there now, to check it out, perhaps find a hiding place, but usually an adult came along.

Uncle Brooke sat on the edge of his lawn chair. He wore white shorts and a bright orange short-sleeved shirt. On his dark, curly hair sat his favorite cap, the lavender one with the rainbow flag. His arm rested on Mom's shoulder. He, Pat and Mom were talking in low voices. Lee kicked some pebbles, jumped up and moved farther away from the fire.

Walking over to Alex, Lee threw a pebble against a big rock.

"Let's split," she mumbled. "Go to the homestead."

"Sure, you ask. Your mom might let us." Alex grinned, but looked embarrassed. Uncle Brooke always wanted to be sure things were totally safe before he let them do anything.

When Lee announced that she and Alex were going for a walk, Uncle Brooke asked predictably, "Where are you going?"

Alex sighed.

At least his dad cares, Lee thought. "Up the hill. We won't be long," she said encouragingly.

"I don't know if...." Uncle Brooke started, taking his cap off and rubbing his forehead.

"They're both eleven now. They'll be fine," Lee's mother interrupted.

"Well...don't stay too long," Uncle Brooke said. "Put on some sun block and bug spray."

"I already did," Alex yelled. He ran along the beach to the trail head, his blond curls bouncing with each step.

"Lee, wear your shoes," Mom said.

"Wait," Lee called after Alex. She slipped her socks and shoes on, rubbed bug repellent on her face, legs and arms and hurried after Alex. He was way ahead and not slowing down at all.

Lee ran up the first part of the old trail. It was steep,

overgrown with branches and roots, and had many wide switchbacks. Alex had disappeared around a bend.

Lee stopped, and with her hands cupped around her mouth she yelled, "Wait for me." No answer. She ran on, out of breath. Jumping over a big root, Lee's left foot caught and she pitched forward, her hands spread in front of her. "Ah-h-h-h," she cried as her head hit a rock. Soon all she saw before her eyes were blue and black swirls, the tree tops and dark skies....

Slowly light broke through the blackness and she began to see cloudy swirls, brighter swirls, sapphire blue curls and circles. Sound returned. Then light. Feelings came back. There was a tingling behind her eyes. A headache. It felt as if her temples were being squeezed between two giant logs.

She opened her eyes a little, but the sun shone so brightly, she briefly closed them again. Moving her hand to her forehead, she felt a lump forming above her eyebrow.

She slowly opened her eyes again. The bright swirls got bigger. The forest light blended the greens together into trees, swaying against the blue sky. Lee sat up. Alex wasn't anywhere to be seen. He must still be running up the hill. Fine. Let him go on alone, she thought. She didn't even want to call out to him.

After a while the pain became less intense. She felt

the lump again, but didn't think it was bleeding. No blood showed on her fingertips or in her brown hair, draped in front of her eyes.

When Alex didn't come back, Lee slowly stood up and started down the hill. By the time she reached the beach, her head had cleared. But what was this?

The camp was at the edge of the trees. In front of it was a dim fire. Or...was it a fire? Lee saw smoke. She rubbed her eyes. Instead of two campers she saw only one, but it was a trailer, a strange contraption, unlike any trailer Lee had ever seen.

"What are you doing?"

Lee whirled around, startled, and put her hand to her head.

"I fell," she told Alex, who stood before her, a puzzled look on his face.

"What's that?" He pointed to the campsite.

Lee tensed. "You mean, you see it too?"

Alex nodded. "That's the gonkiest trailer I've ever seen. What's that green and brown thing by the smoke?"

"I don't know. It's alive. It moved." Lee took a few steps down the beach.

Alex followed. "We must be camped around the bend or something," he said. "I don't get it. I thought we could see our camp from here. And this...this...gonky set-up wasn't here when we left." He frowned, his grey eyes narrowing in concentration.

"Let's walk around it, back to our camp," Lee said, touching her head again. "This lump hurts."

The creature by the smoke screeched. Its chain rattled. The animal turned its back to the fire, sidling up to the warmth. Two eyes gazed at them while it called, "Woo, woo, woo."

"It has a little face," Alex whispered, staring.

"It's a monkey." Lee took several steps forward. "Come on Alex. It's cute. Look at its bright little eyes, and it's wearing a little dark-green dress."

They hurried across the beach until they got to within a few steps of the monkey.

"It might be wild." Alex hesitated.

The monkey looked at them, turning her eyes from one face to the other. She sat chained to a low bench, her behind warmed by glowing coals between two bricks. On the bricks sat a grate and a steaming kettle of water.

"Do you think I could pet it?" Lee's headache was completely forgotten. The monkey fascinated her. She wanted to touch it, pick it up, but caution stopped her. What if it scratched, or bit? The monkey called, "Woo, woo," then yawned, the inside of her mouth showing rows of sharp little teeth.

"Better watch out," Alex warned. "My dad doesn't like me going to strangers' places." He backed up a few steps.

From inside the trailer first one dog, then several dogs, began barking. A woman's voice called to them to quiet down. They continued their ruckus. Someone with a heavy step walked around inside. The trailer wobbled, shaking the patched tarps that hung like a sagging old tent off one side. A sheet, pillow case and dish towel quivered on a line that hung under an awning on the opposite wall. A broom, leaning against the wall by the door, fell over.

Slowly, with a loud squeak, the door of the trailer swung open. Lee and Alex stood rooted to their spot as several small, brown dogs streaked out. They tumbled over each other in their excitement at sniffing and jumping up at strange legs.

In the doorway stood a heavy, short woman with blue-grey eyes in a round face. A black band around her head held a net over her hair. Wild, frizzy tufts of grey hair stuck out at both sides, hiding her ears. She wore a dress that hung down to her calves. Or was it a night gown? No, it was a dress, made of the same green material as the monkey's. The woman looked about as old as Natasha's grandmother.

With a wriggling little dog under one arm, she teetered for a second on the threshold. Regaining her balance, she set one foot, in a flat, heavy shoe, down on a lower step.

"I'm glad you got here." Her voice was warm but stern.

The woman called the dogs back before she said, "Woo messed up the trailer. That's why she's out here."

Unhooking the monkey's chain, she cuddled the little animal in her arms. "You naughty thing." She stroked her pet, saying, "She's usually very good."

Lee glanced at Alex, then looked at the woman. "When did *you* get here?" she asked.

"A few days ago. I'm here for my usual fall outing. I've been expecting you. Your father said you'd come for a lesson some day."

Alex looked as puzzled as Lee felt, his mouth gaping in surprise. "A lesson on what?" he said.

"Don't be smart, boy. Did you bring easels? I guess not." The woman disappeared behind the tarp flap. Lee could hear her rummaging around.

"She's nuts. Let's get out of here," Alex whispered.

They ran along the beach for a few feet before Lee stopped.

"It's all changed." Scratching her head, she remembered her lump. Even though it no longer throbbed, when she touched the area, it hurt.

Alex whistled through his gapped front teeth. "Man, this is really gonky. The trees are gone. It looks like somebody logged here."

Lee nodded. "We should've passed our campsite by now. There's the dirt road," she pointed, hardly believing her eyes. They'd come down here every summer for as long as she could remember, but she'd never seen this area. Some tall, skinny trees reached high up into the air. Shrubs and dead branches covered the rest of the ground. Lee saw stumps, stumps of what must have been huge, old trees, with roots like the one Lee had fallen over, but bigger, much bigger. Some stumps had been pulled up, leaving huge holes.

"I don't get it," Alex said. "Did we miss our campsite?"

"I think so. It's almost like...." Lee didn't want to say it. She didn't even want to think it. But from the old homestead trail to their camp was the same distance as.... She slapped at a mosquito on her arm. "That woman," she said hesitantly, "her trailer is in our spot."

"That's what I thought." Alex sat down.

"So, where are they?" Lee sat beside him on a stump as big around as a table.

"How should I know?" Alex muttered.

How could everything be gone, as if by magic?

"This is stupid." Lee smacked the stump with her heal and glared at Alex.

"Don't get mad at me," he said.

"I'm not." Lee jumped up. "Let's ask her."

"That woman? No way." Alex shook his head, shocked.

"She's all right. She'll know where our campsite is. She's been here for a few days." Lee frowned. "I wonder why we didn't see her before."

"You go." Alex stayed on the stump, but by the time Lee reached the beach she heard him running after her.

"Let's check for tire marks." He pointed to the old dirt road.

The path leading from the paved road down to the beach was barely wide enough for Uncle Brooke's big motorhome. No fresh marks showed, even though they had only driven here yesterday. It rained last night. Little rivulets showed where the water had run from the

31

puddles to the beach. There were no signs of traffic.

"Remember that little tree? The one that always scrapes the roof?" Alex asked.

"It's gone!" Lee walked along the side of the road. Someone had cut the big trees here too, leaving only their stumps. The tracks looked wider, as wide as a regular road. But Lee didn't see a single tire mark anywhere.

They searched the dirt road for some distance before turning back to the beach. No tire marks showed there either.

"Isn't this where your dad almost got stuck?" Lee pointed. "There should be a pothole, but...." She swatted a fly on her cheek.

"Dad hasn't come along here since it rained. That's for sure!" Alex walked ahead, searching for signs. He was moving in the direction of their camp– the woman's camp.

"Let's ask her." Lee caught up with him.

"I don't know." Alex slowly shook his head. "What did she mean about our easels?" He twisted his foot back and forth in some pebbles.

"Beats me," Lee shrugged.

"Let's spy on her," Alex said.

"I'm going to talk to her." Lee walked along the beach. Alex followed.

The woman sat on a stool outside the trailer. She, and the monkey on her lap, stared at them as they walked closer. The strange, wire-haired dogs bounded up again to sniff their shoes and legs. One of them snapped at Lee's shoe.

"Come back," the woman called. "No, Pout. Come."

The snapping dog looked at her, then ran back and lay at her feet. The others followed.

"Don't worry, they're friendly. They're Belgian griffons. I used to breed them. I don't so much any more." The woman stroked the dog called Pout. "Your dad said you might be curious. He said you don't get away much." She studied them. "You can't be identical twins." She tapped one finger on her lips and nodded. "You do look a little alike. Same small noses, same high foreheads, but different mouths. Yours is much wider." She pointed to Alex. "You have a nice, strong chin," she said to Lee. "You seem strong-willed and independent. And you're taller."

"We're *not* twins." Lee swallowed hard. "Can you tell us where our campsite is? It's around here somewhere. We have two motorhomes."

"Motorhomes? What are those?"

"Vans. Trailers, like yours. But newer," Alex said.

The woman shook her head. "All that's around here for miles and miles is beach. And gravel. And rocks. And trees. And your place up there." She pointed up the hill towards the homestead. "This is the only campsite. I'm the only one staying here. Come, get your paints ready." She walked over to the tarp and disappeared behind the flap.

As she did, Lee noticed their sliding rock, just behind her trailer.

Lee nudged Alex. "Look," she whispered. "The slide."

Alex gasped. "This *is* our spot." He looked around. "The trees are bigger over there. The beach is kind of different too. But the climbing rocks are exactly the same. Man...."

He held the tarp flap aside and asked the woman, "Do you know another beach around here with a sliding rock like that one?"

"No. Take this." The woman handed him a can of paint and a stick. "Stir," she commanded. "We *will* paint today, or my name isn't Emily Carr. Enough of your distractions."

"You're Emily Carr?" Lee looked into the tent.

The woman poured paint into another can and gave it to Lee. "Stir," she said, turning away and walking to a large stack of manila paper. Attaching a sheet to a board, she carried it out into the sunshine. Again she disappeared into the tent.

Lee moved over to Alex and set her paint can down beside his on the sand. "Emily Carr!" she whispered. "She's a famous painter. My new teacher was just talking about her. But she didn't tell me Emily Carr lived around here, or that she was so strange."

For a moment Lee wished she could stay and paint. She loved the reds and browns, was tempted to put her fingers into them.

A thunderous crash broke the silence. Lee breathed in sharply and swung around, almost overturning the can of paint. "What was...?"

"Something fell," Alex said, his eyes bulging. "Something huge! Up there." He pointed to the hill behind them.

After a few more crackling sounds the air became very still. No dogs barked. No birds sang. Even the wind hushed.

Emily Carr came out of the tent and looked up at the hill, where the homestead was hidden behind the trees.

"Goodness, another one dead," she muttered. "Too many. Your folks are getting greedy." She shook her head. "Every day this goes on. I'll have to move the elephant."

"The elephant?" Lee and Alex asked at the same time. First a monkey, now an elephant. Was Emily Carr part of a circus? Did she do disappearing acts?

"The trailer," she said, waving her hand in its direction. "My summer home. I call her the elephant." She walked back into the tent. While they stirred, Lee and Alex whispered about what to do. This had to be the right beach, but their parents were gone. The fire pit was in a different place. The canoe, the clothes line, even the tubes had disappeared. In its place were Emily Carr and an old trailer she called the elephant. She thought they were twins who lived up on the hill. A loud crashing sound meant another one was dead.

"Another what?" Lee wanted to know. "A fallen tree maybe?"

Alex shrugged, a worried look on his face. He wanted to go up the hill to investigate.

Leaving the paints on the sand, they ran along the beach and started up the trail, but it was different too. The ground had been leveled and some roots that grew across the path had been flattened in places. Stumps were sprinkled with bits of sawdust. This wasn't the *old* trail; this was a *new* road.

The trees alongside the path showed big gashes in the trunks, as if something heavy had bumped into them. Pieces of bark were missing. The dirt showed marks as if something had been dragged uphill.

"Let's hurry." Lee was ahead of Alex this time and she had forgotten all about the lump on her head.

After rushing up the trail, Lee slowed down and caught her breath. She recognized the road as the trail they had climbed dozens of times. It had the same curves, the same lookouts, the same views of the Strait of Georgia waters and the Gulf islands. But the trees were enormous. Lee shivered in the silence. On the forest floor grew bushes and brambles so dense Lee was sure she couldn't make her way through it if she wanted to.

"This morning I waited here for you." Alex pointed to a boulder at Lookout Point. "I sat on this rock." He sat down. "These trees were smaller. I'm sure!" He slapped his arm, then his calf. "There are more mosquitoes and they're biting."

Lee glanced around and moved over to Alex. "Something weird is going on," she whispered. "I don't like it."

Alex nodded, making room for Lee on the boulder. They sat side by side, whispering. Lee said there were no tire tracks here, so she'd like to go back to ask Emily Carr more questions. Alex wanted to hike to the homestead and The Bluff, where they could see the whole beach below. He had to find out what a "dead one" was, he said. They both jumped as another crash broke the silence. The noise was closer this time, much closer, coming from just up ahead on the road.

"That wasn't a falling tree. Something bumped into something," Lee whispered, her heart pounding against her ribcage.

Quietly, they walked up the road side by side, moving slowly, peering ahead through the trees, looking over their shoulders and to the sides, ready to duck.

Alex held out his hand. "Listen," he whispered.

Lee had heard it too– a crash, then the sound of something big rubbing against a tree. A man's voice yelled, "Left, left!"

"Someone's coming down the road," Lee whispered. "Hide."

Alex crouched behind an enormous root.

Lee jumped off the road after him. A man leading two large, brown horses came around the bend. The animals, in harnesses, strained and pulled, their hooves kicking dirt into the air.

"Sharper turn," came the low voice of another man still hidden by the curve in the road.

The lead man shouted at the horses, moving the team sideways, then forward a step. The chains behind them became taut. Lee stood up in her hiding place to see what would come next, but then ducked down quickly to avoid being seen.

"A log," Alex whispered. He had a peephole between two roots so he could see the road.

Lee nudged him to move over so she could see. The chains were attached to a section of log. The front end of the log had been cut into a curve, to look like the front part of a ski. It glided around the corner and down the road like a huge single runner on a sleigh.

The log smashed into a tree as it rounded the bend, bark scraping off with a screech. The horses kept pulling. The log righted itself so that it pointed straight down the road.

The second man came into view. He walked beside a wooden sled that was tied to the end of the log and bumped along in the dust. As the log started to slide faster down the hill, the man pushed an old anchor from the sled onto the road. This slowed the log, so it couldn't pick up speed and slide into the horses' hind legs.

"Whoa," the front man yelled, holding the reins. Everyone stopped. The men pried the anchor loose with metal bars and pushed it back onto the sled. The horses continued.

As the horses came closer, Lee caught their smell and saw their powerful muscles straining, their bodies sweating, foam dripping from their mouths. Their big, hairy feet pawed at the dirt as they pulled the log over a flattened tree root.

"Whoa." The front man slacked the reins he'd been holding tightly.

The horses breathed heavily. One of them snorted and looked over at where Lee and Alex lay hidden in a hollow behind the mass of roots. The horse's breath wafted toward them. Lee flattened herself against the earth and stayed still.

The second man took a canteen from the sled. Both men took their hats off and wiped their sweaty foreheads with big, red handkerchiefs. When they poured water into the hats, the horses whinnied. The men held the hats full of water up to the animals. They sucked as they drank, their tails swatting at the clouds of insects on their rumps.

The men put their hats back on, took turns drinking water from the canteen and tied it back onto the sled. They sat down on stumps along the road. The lead man pulled a small metal box from his heavy wool pants' pocket. He took out something brown for each of them. They popped it into their mouths and started chewing. The other man rubbed his arm.

"Does it hurt still, John?" the first man asked. He wiped his face again with his handkerchief, leaving a streak of dirt across one cheek.

"Just a little. We'll have to be more careful tonight." His stubbled chin showed, but the top part of his face was hidden by the hat's wide brim. He spit a small stream of brown juice onto the road.

"I hope the water's calm."

"That woman worries me," John said. "I saw her drawing tree stumps."

A small trickle of brown juice ran down the other man's chin. "She's that painter," he said, wiping his face.

"She *says* she's a painter. But I don't know," John shrugged. "She's awful strange. I don't like her snooping around. She walked up to our place with a pack of dogs, looked around, shook her head 'nd left. She didn't say a word."

"She's all right."

"What if she talks?" John insisted.

"I'll make sure she won't." He snapped his suspenders against the front of his heavy plaid shirt, making two small clouds of dust. "Giddap," he said, taking the reins.

The horses pulled and snorted. Their flanks quivered as they moved their load slowly forward. John kicked the log with one of his heavy, laced boots before he walked down the hill beside the sled.

John and the sled had rounded the next bend before Lee and Alex got up, scratching their mosquito bites.

"Let's look around while they're gone." Alex pointed up the hill.

After following the road for a short while, Lee heard whacking sounds, as if someone was chopping wood. She pulled Alex's sleeve and put her finger to her lips. He nodded. They moved carefully from tree to tree, making sure not to step on twigs.

Lee and Alex froze in their tracks. In a large clearing stood the homestead shacks, but the walls no longer had holes. The creepers and shrubs were gone. Grass and weeds grew around the shacks. The small window frame in the larger shack held a pane of glass. A black stove pipe stuck out of a wall.

They crept a few steps closer to the fire pit in front of the shacks. Crouching behind a shrub, they looked at the thin wisps of smoke coming from the pit.

"Like Emily Carr's," Lee whispered, pointing to the grill with a kettle.

Some blackened pots and dishes lay by the small creek that ran beside the fire pit. A tall, wooden fence protected one area. When Lee crept closer, she saw it was a garden with corn, carrots, lettuce and other plants in rows. There were even some new, small apple trees across the creek, where the big, older ones used to be. They were fenced off as well.

Farther back stood an outhouse. Someone had strung a clothes line between the smaller shack and the outhouse. On it hung two rags and an old, faded blouse.

The people that moved into the homestead had worked fast. Lee and Alex were here only two weekends ago, picking green apples off the old trees and telling ghost stories.

Two children, looking so much alike they had to be twins, slowly pulled a huge saw with a wooden handle on each end through a felled tree, back and forth, back and forth. To be high enough to reach the saw handles, the children stood on wooden boxes. Even though they had only cut a short way through the trunk, they looked tired, or bored.

The boy wore pants that came to just below his knees. Two patches were sown onto the seat. The girl had on a dress that hung down to her calves. Both children wore long stockings.

Farther along on the same felled tree stood a small woman. She swung a double-bladed axe above her head and down on a branch with a thud.

Alex nudged Lee. "Let's explore," he whispered, pointing to the shacks, their doors wide open.

"I don't know. It's too buggy. No wonder they're wearing all those clothes."

"We might find evidence." Alex crawled through the bush along the edge of the clearing.

Evidence of what? Lee wanted to ask. She hadn't seen any tire marks coming up here. But she didn't say anything and followed Alex into the bigger shack.

In one corner stood a metal barrel on a stand, with a door in the front and a stove pipe in the back, connected to the wall. In another corner stood a bed with a pile of sheets on the mattress. By the wall lay two more small mattresses with blankets. In the middle of the shack, on a table made of planks and logs, stood an old-fashioned lantern, the kind that used gas or oil. Apparently, there was no electricity. Five rough chairs, made from blocks and strips of wood, stood around the table. From the ceiling hung a skinny, yellow strip of paper with a small roll dangling at the bottom of it. Dozens of flies were stuck to the strip, but hundreds more flew around the room.

A set of shelves, built from logs and planks, stood along a wall. Lee walked over to look at the books and newspapers. She picked up a book that said *Holy Bible,* then put it back and flipped through a photo album.

Many pictures were of babies, by themselves or two together. They wore the same knitted bonnets and sweaters, one blue, the other pink. One photo showed a man and a woman in old-fashioned clothing, holding the two tiny babies. They stood proudly in front of a house and flat farm lands that reached far back to the horizon.

Lee wandered to another shelf. It held jars of beans, dried apples, flour, salt or sugar and tea. There were some cooking utensils and candles. Beside it stood a wooden box made into a doll house. Some paper dolls and clothes lay in it. Lee saw a small box of paints and a brush as well. She thought again about painting with Emily Carr. Part of her wanted to go back down the hill to talk to the painter. She felt excited about having met her, felt almost as if she'd somehow known her before.

Lee looked around the room. She didn't want to touch anything else on the shelves. Two weeks ago this place had been empty, old and creaky. Were these people ghosts come alive, the ghosts she and Alex had made up in their stories? She shivered.

"What are we looking for anyway?" she whispered. "None of our stuff is up here. Let's go to the beach."

"How could everything change like this?" Alex frowned.

They sneaked out of the shack. The woman and the twins were still hard at work, so Alex convinced Lee to come and peek into the smaller shack. It was empty except for some bedding, a pair of pants and a shirt hanging on nails, a lantern hanging from a nail in a ceiling beam, a big wooden tub standing in a corner and an accordion lying on a box in another corner.

Lee felt more uncomfortable. They were snooping. People really lived here.

She froze. A noise came through the back wall of the small shack– a scraping noise. They rushed outside and lay down in the tall weeds by the side wall.

"Check it out." Alex pointed, his mouth right beside Lee's ear.

Lee shrugged, crawling ahead on her elbows and knees. She giggled. "A goat."

A white nanny rubbed her head back and forth on the wall of a small lean-to built onto the back of the shack. The rope she was tied to had wound around a stake so often that the goat could only just reach the wall of the lean-to with her head. She looked at the children and bleated. A fluffed-up mother hen strutted from the lean-to, leading a string of five chicks.

Lee crawled around the corner and stood up. From here the twins and their mother could not see her. She petted the animal and untangled the rope.

"I don't know about goats, but my friend Roy's *horse* could never eat this much grass in two weeks." Alex shook his head, looking at the large, almost bare patches. The hen clucked her chicks away from him toward the tall trees. "These people couldn't have such a big pile of compost in two weeks either." He scratched a mosquito bite on his neck. "Not if they're *normal* people!"

"Let's talk to them," Lee said. "Maybe they can

explain." She looked around the corner of the shack.

Just at that moment the woman's boot slipped on the log. The axe she had swung high over her head came down with a thud on her leg. She screamed and fell off the trunk. The twins screamed as well. "Ma! Ma!" the girl yelled.

Lee gasped. She ran through the clearing, jumped over the creek and crouched beside the woman's head.

"Who are you?" the girl asked, obviously surprised but distracted by her mother's cries. The boy was already bent over her leg.

The woman lay moaning, her eyes closed.

"Ma!" The girl pulled the heavy pant leg up to the knee. The boy started untying the string that was used as a boot lace.

"She's bleeding a lot," the girl said.

"We'll have to stop the blood." The boy pulled the string from the boot and tied it around his mother's leg, above the cut. "I'll hold it. Get a tourniquet." He swatted the flies away.

The girl rushed to the shack. A few minutes later she returned with a strip of cloth and a stick. While the boy unwound the string, the girl wrapped the cloth around the leg, again above the cut. Putting the stick through the cloth, she twisted. The flow of blood stopped to a trickle.

How had the twins known what to do? Lee wondered. They couldn't be any older than she or Alex, but they seemed so sure. They needed water now, to clean the cut. Getting up, Lee saw Alex standing by the creek. He was never very good with injuries and he hated the sight of blood.

"Bring some water," she called to him.

"Sterilize it first," the boy said.

"Sterilize?" Lee wasn't sure what he meant.

"Boil it," the girl said.

"How?" Lee asked.

"On the fire." The boy looked at her curiously, taking his dirty checkered cap off. He wiped his forehead with his shirt sleeve, showing a tanned wrist and hand, but white skin where his sleeve normally covered his arm.

"Who are you?" the girl repeated.

Everyone said their names before the boy, Willard, helped Lee rekindle the fire. Alex filled the kettle with water. The girl, Clare, stayed with her mother, who cried out in pain.

When they had cleaned the leg and put an old, folded blanket under the mother's head, Willard said, "We'll have to put iodine on it. It'll sting, Ma." The woman nodded.

He ran to the larger shack and returned with a small bottle of rusty-coloured liquid. Carefully he poured some on the cut, staining the leg. The mother's eyes were closed, but Lee saw her mouth grimace in pain for a moment. Beads of sweat formed on her face.

"We need an ambulance. Phone 911," Alex called, standing back by the creek again.

"Do you have a phone?" Lee looked at the questioning

faces of the twins.

"911?" Clare said, her eyebrows raised.

"I guess not," Lee said. Looking at the woman on the ground, she said, "Your mother needs to go to a hospital."

Willard stood between his mother and Lee. "She's staying here." He looked at his sister.

"She needs help." Lee felt a bubble of unease creeping up from her stomach. "She can't stay here. We need a doctor, or someone from a rescue team."

When the woman made a sound, everyone turned back to her.

"We're here, Ma." Clare kneeled by her mother's head. She wiped the pale face with a wet handkerchief before loosening the tourniquet. She tightened it again when blood started to flow heavily.

"Ma, d'you need a doctor?" Clare asked.

"No." The woman shook her head slightly. "We can't pay. I'll be fine." Pain flashed across her face while she talked.

"We can give him corn for coming up here," Willard said. "Or the hen. The chicks, they're old enough now. He can come up with Pa. I can run down 'nd tell him."

"No." The woman shook her head more firmly.

"You'd better go," Clare said, getting up. "We don't want to upset Ma. Don't make trouble."

"Trouble? She needs stitches." Lee looked at the cut in the leg. It was at least twice as big as the cut on her friend Janet's arm when she tripped on the bicycle rack at school, and Janet had needed a dozen stitches. The principal had taken her to the doctor in his car. "She needs help." Lee was determined. She walked over to the woman.

But Clare stopped her. "Leave Ma alone."

Lee felt the girl's strong hands pushing on her arms. She looked at the flashing brown eyes in the tanned face. Clare was worried.

"If we help you, we can get her to the shack," Lee said. Maybe she could show these kids that she and Alex were only trying to help.

"They're cabins, not shacks," Willard said, glaring at Lee, his hands on his hips.

The woman grimaced as she tried to sit up. She fell back onto the blanket.

The twins agreed that their mother couldn't stay where she was. They decided to bring a mattress over and carry her back on it.

"Get Uncle John's," Willard said, starting toward the smaller cabin.

"That man, John, is your uncle?" Alex asked.

"You saw him?" Willard glanced at his sister.

When Alex told the twins about the two men and the log, Clare said, "The other man's our pa. D'you think we can get him to come back?" she asked Willard.

The boy shook his head. "They started late. They've to get everything afloat 'nd chained down before the tide's out. It'll be dark before they get their haul to the city."

"What haul?" Lee's hands tightened into fists. She wanted to ask a million questions. Did the twins know where Mom, Uncle Brooke and Pat were? Why didn't they want someone to come up here to help their mother? It couldn't just be because they were poor.

Lee didn't get an answer to her questions, because Clare and Willard ran off to the smaller cabin. She and Alex followed.

In the tiny, dark room they pulled a mattress out from under the heap of bedding. The four of them struggled to hold the mattress up high while they crossed the creek. Both Lee and Alex got their shoes wet. Lee wished she had bigger arm muscles. She could tell that the twins carried their burden more easily.

Willard lowered the mattress. "I'm gonna get a drink," he said, wiping his forehead.

Laying the mattress down, both Willard and Clare crouched by the creek to scoop water in their cupped hands.

"You'll get sick," Alex said. "Beaver fever."

"What?" Willard frowned, then slurped up another handful.

"We drink it all the time," Clare said.

Lee was parched. Her tongue felt as dry as a blackboard brush. But Uncle Brooke always warned against drinking water straight from creeks. He said it had diseases. Clare slurped again before splashing water on her face. "Ah," she sighed.

Scooping up a handful, Lee looked closely at the clear, cool water. She splashed her face and slurped up a little to wet the inside of her dry mouth. It was icy cold and tasted different from bottled water. She scooped up another handful, spilling most of it down her shirt before she got it to her mouth.

They picked up the mattress and continued. When they got closer to where the twins' mother had been lying behind the log, they gasped in horror. The mattress fell to the ground.

"Oh no. Ma!" Willard cried.

A trail of blood led along the grass to the end of the log. The woman sat there holding her leg.

"Ma, you shouldn't have moved," Clare said. She checked her mother's leg. "It's bleeding more."

"You need stitches," Lee said. "We'll get Uncle Brooke and...." She stopped, then asked, "Do you know where our parents are?"

"Are there more of you?" The woman asked. She grimaced as Clare tightened the tourniquet again. "That painter and all her animals, are you with her?"

"No. Our parents were camped at the beach, but now they're gone," Alex said. "Do you know where they are?"

The twins shook their heads.

Willard turned to Alex. "Let's cut poles to put under the mattress. That way we can carry Ma back to the cabin."

Lee nodded. She didn't understand why the twins

weren't trying harder to get help. They hadn't even bandaged the cut. Perhaps they didn't have bandages. The flies that crawled on the woman's leg might infect the wound.

"Do you have any bug spray?" she asked, scratching her neck.

Clare shrugged. "Never heard of it," she mumbled. Looking up at Lee, she said, "Oh, you mean fly tox? No, we don't use it."

"My uncle knows a lot about first aid. If you know where the campers are...." Lee tried again.

Clare was bent over her mother. She shrugged.

"Campers," Lee continued. "One's a big, new, white motorhome with a blue awning. The other, my mom's, is a really old Volkswagen van. And there's a canoe. But everything is gone. Even the tubes." Suddenly Lee realized just how scary her situation was. She sat down on the ground, feeling shaky.

"You've all that?" Clare looked at Lee's T-shirt, her shorts and runners. Then her eyes rested on Lee's watch. "You must be rich."

"No, we're not." Lee stopped. They were all gone! She looked around the clearing, almost expecting Uncle Brooke or Mom to come walking from behind a shrub, as they had done when they played hide and seek up here.

Clare checked her mother's leg and wiped her forehead. "The droughts, weren't you hit by them?"

"The droughts?" Lee wasn't sure just what a drought

was.

"The dust storms, the droughts?" Clare sounded amazed.

Lee shrugged. "What's that?"

Clare's mother must have been listening. She opened her eyes. "You don't know about the droughts?" she asked.

"It didn't rain for several years," Clare said. "We'd no water. The wells dried up. All the plants died. We couldn't even wash. Then the wind blew 'nd blew. It made big dust storms. There was sand in my eyes 'nd my ears. In our food. In my bed. And piles of sand by the doors 'nd windows. Pa, he used a shovel 'nd wheelbarrow to dump the sand back outside." She swatted at the flies on her mother's leg.

Lee wondered if Clare was telling the truth. "A wheelbarrow?" she grinned.

"Really," Clare said. Her mother nodded.

Clare continued. "The dust clouds, they were so big, it was dark even during the day. I guess you never lived on the prairies."

Lee shook her head.

"Then grasshoppers came," Clare went on. "There were millions. You'd see black clouds of 'em from the window. They ate everything, the washing on the clothesline, the fence posts, the trees. Nothing left."

Lee heard Clare's mother sigh. The woman looked so sad, tears shone in her eyes. That's how Mom had looked after Dad's garage sale. "There's nothing left," she'd said. But at least she and Mom had their place. And a fridge and stove and clothes that weren't patched, and beds, dressers, a couch, a phone, a TV, so many things compared to this family.

Clare's voice broke into Lee's thoughts. "....got laid off from his job 'nd the bank took our farm. We had a real nice farm in Saskatchewan. We put our things on our wagon."

She loosened the tourniquet on her mother's leg, but tightened it as the blood started to flow again.

"Our two horses, they were so skinny we thought they'd fall over dead. But they pulled our wagon–slowly. We left for Regina where Ma...."

Her mother gave a short cry. "No, Clare."

"I wasn't gonna tell, Ma." Clare bent over the cut leg, her face turning red.

"I'm fine now," the woman said. "Thank you for your help. You two'd better go home." She nodded at Lee and Alex.

"But we can't find our campsite. Emily Carr is there. With her elephant." Lee got up.

"Her elephant?" Clare looked up, her face still flushed.

"Her trailer. She calls it that. It's old and wobbly."

"The painter." Clare smiled. "She's good. She comes in the spring 'nd the fall. Pa wants us to take lessons, for our schooling. We haven't had anything to trade yet. Pa's hoping she'll take some corn. He said her sister died just last month, so we have to wait a while before we go to talk to her. Pa says she likes to be alone a lot."

Alex and Willard arrived with four poles. They made a make-shift stretcher with the mattress. At first their mother wouldn't hear of being carried back to the cabin. She got up and tried to walk, leaning her bony arms on her children's shoulders. But the cut started bleeding heavily. She mumbled something about being busy and clumsy, but lay down on the stretcher.

The four children carried the woman to the creek. They managed to get her across it and to the larger cabin.

Lee took Alex outside. "They've got a secret," she whispered. "Something we're not supposed to know, about Regina."

Alex's eyes narrowed. "They're weird man."

"Shhh." Lee put her finger across her lips.

Alex continued in a whisper. "Remember how that painter said they were getting greedy? She meant these people." He moved his hands back and forth excitedly. "Let's go." He pulled her arm.

"Where?" Lee asked.

"To stop them." Alex was anxious to be off. "Find out what they're doing. Maybe they have Dad, and Pat and your mom. Aren't you worried?"

"Of course!" Lee walked to the creek and sat down by the gurgling water.

"Do you think...?" She didn't want to say the rest out loud. She wondered if Dad was involved. Of course not, she told herself. He might have sold things and used all of Mom's money for himself, but he wasn't a criminal. "He wouldn't...." she mumbled.

"What?" Alex said.

"My dad. He wouldn't be part of...." Lee pointed at the cabin.

Alex's eyebrows shot up. "No way," he said. Pat says your dad can't be trusted, but...." He shook his head.

Lee remembered what she'd written in her journal about living in the woods. She looked around. "Could you live like this, in these shacks, I mean cabins?"

Alex shook his head. "We won't have to. Let's find those guys with the log."

Lee suggested they stay around and talk to the twins instead. Alex agreed, reluctantly.

"But," he said, sounding very sure of himself, "if that doesn't work, I'm going down there."

"Let's try the saw," Lee suggested. "Make a bunch of noise. Maybe someone will come outside."

"It looks hard," Alex said. "I guess they don't have a chain saw."

They stepped up onto the boxes on either side of the fallen tree. Grabbing the handles, Lee yelled "Pull" while she pushed. At first the saw bent and wobbled and stuck. But as they yelled at each other and wriggled and lifted the saw a bit, it slowly ground its way across the wood to Alex. It was Lee's turn to pull it back.

Willard came out of the cabin. "What're you doing

that for?"

Alex grinned at Lee. "Just helping out," he called over his shoulder. "It's hard though."

"You'll hurt yourselves that way." Willard jumped across the creek. "Here, watch." He showed Alex how to move the big crosscut saw, standing behind the handle and away from the sharp teeth. "Put your feet down firmly," he said.

"Are you building another cabin?" Alex asked.

Willard pushed and pulled the saw. "No. Here, you cut 'nd I'll show her." Willard jumped down, walked to the other side and helped Lee.

"Are you selling this log in Regina?" Lee wanted Willard to talk about the details that would fill the gaps in their story.

"Regina?" Willard looked surprised. "No. That's a long way."

"But you lived there." Lee wasn't giving up easily.

"Not very long. Were you there?" As he said that, Willard glanced sideways at Lee and jerked the saw.

Lee thought hard. Something was in Regina that worried this family, or at least something had happened there. If she said she had never been to Regina, Willard might stop talking. If she acted suspicious, he might wonder if she knew something, whatever that might be. He might talk.

"Uhmmm..." she looked directly at the boy, her eyes wide open. "I might know about it," she added, nodding her head.

No one spoke. The saw scraped back and forth, adding to the small pile of sawdust. Nervously Lee clenched and unclenched her sweaty hands. She waited, watching Willard closely, hoping he would say something that would help her find Mom. He pulled and pushed the saw, his face grim.

He turned briefly and said, "Did you see...?"

Lee nodded harder, wondering what she was supposed to have seen, but trying to look sure of herself.

Willard stopped pulling the saw. "So, you came up here for that?" He jumped down. "What d'you want? The money?" His voice became a whisper. "Are you gonna turn her in?" He stood in front of Lee, his hands tightening to fists, the knuckles turning white. She saw sweat on his forehead. He wiped at it angrily when it ran into his eyes. "Well?" he said, stepping even closer.

"We won't turn her in." Lee's mind raced. Turn who in? His mother? For what? Was it something different from what the men were doing with the logs or whatever their haul was?

"Why did she do it?" Lee said, grasping for clues. None of this made sense. None at all!

Willard dropped his fists. "She had to," he said. "Our farm was ruined."

He stopped, but when Lee stared hard at him, he talked quickly. "Pa 'nd Uncle John jumped a freight train from Regina to Vancouver. They heard there was work in British Columbia. They were gonna find jobs. Send us money. We planned to join 'em. Bring the horses."

Willard sat down on the box. Alex walked around the felled tree and sat down beside Lee on the ground. They waited. Willard took his heavy cap off and wiped his face.

"What happened?" Alex rubbed the palms of his hands, red from the hard work.

Willard put his cap back on, pulling it low over his forehead. He talked quickly, but in a whisper. "We didn't hear from Pa for weeks...didn't know if they'd arrived on the west coast. Sometimes the police...they stop the trains. Take 'em to work camps."

"Who?" Lee was confused. Willard talked too fast.

"All the men that get free rides on top of the trains." Willard nodded impatiently. He glanced at Lee and Alex before continuing.

"We'd lived in Regina, on the street, under our wagon. The horses were bedded down on each side. We couldn't find jobs. Ma sold whatever she could. Three weeks later we had nothing left. No food." He rested his head on one fist.

Lee stared. She tried to imagine living on a street under a wagon. She tried to imagine having nothing. What would it be like, asking strangers for jobs?

"Regina sounds awful," she said, emotion choking her voice. She cleared her throat. "Couldn't you go on welfare? My friend's mom is."

"What's welfare?" Willard said.

"I'm not sure. I think it's money the government

gives you." Lee looked at Alex, who nodded his head.

"Free money?" Willard looked up. "Pa, he must know about that. He's good with getting news about money 'nd jobs. Before he jumped the train they gave him twelve cents a day on relief...for all of us. He says things're as bad as ever...all across Canada. Even in Vancouver."

"So why didn't your dad stay with you?" Lee's anger flared. "He left you. With no money? My dad...." She heard her voice getting louder. Clenching her fists angrily, she squeezed hard. She banged her fists down on her knees.

Willard frowned at her and said, "Pa, he did it for us. He told me so when he left. He said he loves us. He does. He 'nd Uncle John, they made all this." He waved his arm at the homestead. "We're doing better. We've warm winter coats. Food every day. Coal oil for the lamps." He smiled. "When Pa comes home from Victoria, he's bringing a rocking chair for Ma 'nd he's buying us a dog, probably from Emily Carr. He's been watching her. He says she's a good dog breeder. But she has too many puppies. She had to trade her big house, the Hill House, for a smaller one, but she's renting it out so she can have some money. She lives in a tiny cottage in Victoria."

Lee watched a beetle crawl away under the tree. Dad had never given them any presents. He'd only taken things from them. "I guess you're lucky," she said, "in a way."

"So what happened in Regina?" Alex swatted at a fly.

Willard gave him a dirty look. His expression changed. Narrowing his eyes, he searched Alex's and Lee's faces. Slowly he said, "You don't really know, d'you? You're just fishing for information. To turn us in. D'you get a reward? You must be real poor, to wanna do that. Who sent you here? Was it Emily Carr? Pa says she's a good painter, but she's real strange. He heard she has her chairs hanging on ropes from the ceiling. She walks around Victoria with a pile of cats and her monkey in a pram and a rat wrapped around her neck. She has birds too. She'd need money to feed all those critters."

Lee smiled at the thought of the painter walking her animals around town. For some reason she felt she needed to defend the painter. "No, it's not her," she said.

"Aw, you don't know." Willard got up.

Lee tried to look as uninterested as possible. She had to call his bluff. Shrugging, she started to get up too. "Fine," she mumbled. "We'll do what we have to then."

"Wait." Willard grabbed her arm. "In the city–Victoria– tomorrow...it's all being fixed. Pa, he's sending money to Regina."

Lee tried hard to hide her confusion. "But why?" she said.

"We were starving. We'd nothing to eat for days. We couldn't find jobs, not even using our horses to pull people's carts." Willard glanced toward the cabin again. "She *had* to steal."

Alex gasped. Lee was shocked as well. The woman had shoplifted. Or had she robbed a bank? They were so poor. They must have hidden since then. No wonder they looked and acted so strangely.

"Did anyone see her?" Alex asked.

"The shopkeeper, he chased her. He almost caught her. But Ma, she crawled underneath a pile of garbage 'nd waited there all day." Willard's voice got softer as he continued. "When it was dark, she came back. We hid under the wagon. In the middle of the night we left."

"We won't tell." A shiver ran down Lee's spine. She couldn't imagine living his life. Then she realized that her own was not so cheery right now either.

"We need to find our parents," she said, searching Willard's face for clues. "Something strange happened at the beach. Can you help?"

Willard looked toward the cabins. Slowly he shook his head. "I can't," he said. "Really, I can't."

"What are your dad and your uncle doing?" Lee asked, jumping up. That unpleasant feeling still hovered in her stomach; these people had more secrets.

"Don't make trouble for us," Willard said, shaking his head. "Ma, she finally stopped having nightmares about rats crawling all over her. Pa's paying for things. I might even go to school next year."

"You don't go to school?" Alex's mouth dropped open. "Lucky," he added, when Willard shook his head.

63

"Don't you *have to* go?" Lee asked.

Willard shrugged. "Pa needs me here."

Lee looked around the clearing. The twins might be lucky to miss worksheets and homework and report cards. But not to go to school at all? To live here in a cabin and cut wood all day? No. She was glad she didn't have to live their life. "Can you read?" she asked.

Willard smiled. "Oh yes. Many words. In Saskatchewan, we went to school before it closed. No money for the teacher." He shrugged, then looked excited again. "Pa teaches us. He found some old newspapers at the dump in the city. And Ma kept a copy of the Farmer's Almanac, 'nd we have the Bible. Pa might take me to see a movie next year. Have you ever seen a movie?" When he saw Lee and Alex nod he said, "Lucky. It costs ten cents. Did you see Laurel and Hardy and Shirley Temple and...?"

"Willard." Clare stood in the cabin's doorway. Her voice sounded anxious as she called, "Ma's feeling worse."

"I shouldn't have told you anything," Willard said. "Ma says I talk too much. Don't turn us in." He ran to the cabin.

"I'm going to find those men," Alex said. "They probably have Dad."

Lee heard the determination in his voice. She knew she couldn't stop him.

The clearing was empty. How could two kids her own age grow up here, never leave, never go into town, live without toys, new books, candy, electricity, TV, friends or their own room? And to think that she had wanted to hide here, alone. She shook her head, as if to clear Willard, Clare and the homestead from her mind.

At the last curve before the beach Alex stopped. Puffing, he sat on a rock. Lee leaned against a tree.

"Now what?" she panted, slapping at and killing the hundredth mosquito.

"We find them," Alex said.

While they rested for a few minutes they made plans: to be seen could be dangerous because, even though Willard had said nice things about his pa, they had to be wary of such a secretive family. After all, who knew what those men might do to get or protect their money?

Lee and Alex hiked to the edge of the forest. Below them lay the beach. The trail made by the horses' hooves and their cargo snaked from the dirt road across the beach and stopped at the tide line. The men and their horses had disappeared. Even the log was gone.

On a camp stool on the sand close to the rocks sat Emily Carr, staring off into the distance. She looked down at the board in her hand and painted something, then stared again. What she saw made her mumble. She sounded upset. Her brush painted quick, angry strokes. She stopped and shook her fist in the direction of the distant beach.

Talking louder now, she painted again, her whole body jerking as she stroked. One of her dogs looked up, then went back to sleep. Several other dogs lay on the beach. Lee counted five of them. The monkey's chain was tied around the woman's waist. Woo slept on a blanket on the sand.

Suddenly the woman yelled, "Enough!" Flinging her brush and board down, she grabbed the monkey into her arms and stomped a few steps along the beach.

One little dog barked excitedly. Two got up, stretched and wagged their tails. The other two stayed where they were.

Turning sharply, she picked up her brush. As she straightened, she saw Lee and Alex.

"You! Get over here. I felt eyes watching me and I knew it wasn't the trees. Look, they're crying! They're bleeding!"

Lee started down the beach toward her. She heard Alex whisper, "Don't! She's crazy."

But Lee kept going. She was fascinated by Emily Carr and wanted to see what she was so angry about.

As she walked closer to the water, Lee could see around a clump of trees and rocks to a long stretch of beach. She and Alex had canoed there on an earlier trip. What she saw now made her stop and stare.

Several huge fires burned farther along the coast. Flames shot up into the air. The fires were so hot they hardly smoked at all.

"Fools," Emily Carr yelled, shaking her fist. "Dratted fools. How dare you cut those beautiful trees, those magnificent giants. Leave them alone," she called, stamping down the beach a ways. "They are my spirits. I *feel* their pain." She turned, hugging the monkey to her, and came over to where Lee was standing.

"First they cut the trees. Now they're burning everything else. I painted there. I painted those trees." She turned to face the fires. "Murderers!" she yelled.

Lee backed up. This angry woman frightened her a little. Mom got upset about clear-cut logging too, but she didn't yell and shake her fist.

She screwed up her courage and said, "Where is my mother?"

Emily Carr looked surprised. "Isn't she at the

cabin? I walked up there once and saw it." Her anger had faded.

"No, no." Lee explained that she wasn't one of the twins. She told the painter who she was and where they were camped this morning.

Emily Carr laughed. "You were camped right here? You *must* have a good imagination. Hold on to it. Adults try hard enough to kill that too."

Lee's hands curled into fists. "I'm not making it up!" A lump formed in her throat and she kicked the gravel. "Where is my mother? We were camped here this morning," she yelled. She kicked again, sending pebbles flying.

"Ah, another fiery temper," Emily Carr chuckled. "Come with me, girl."

Tying the monkey to a tree, she offered Lee some lemonade and flat, dried biscuits with jam, sitting down heavily on a creaking chair to listen as Lee retold her story.

"Speak up girl, I'm a little deaf," she said. She seemed interested, asking, "What time did you leave for your hike? How badly did she cut that leg?" Lee didn't talk about the twins' mother stealing or any other details Willard had shared. When she finished, Emily Carr said quietly, "These are hard times for all of us. Look at you, so strangely dressed– indecently, shamefully. Such bare legs." She shook her head. "I guess you have no money."

Lee looked at her shorts. They were from an old

gym outfit, not *that* short. Why were they shameful? It was still summer– too hot to wear as many clothes as Willard and Clare.

"I don't know what kind of game you're playing," the woman continued. "You may not be who I thought you were but you do seem *almost* familiar. Anyway, you can't stay here with me." She shook her head, pointed up the hill and said, "We'd better check that leg of hers."

Without giving Lee time to say anything more, she went into her trailer. A few minutes later she came back out with a cloth bag.

"I'm not playing games," was all Lee could say.

"Enough talk. Come along," she said, walking off toward the trail with her dogs.

"Alex?" Lee stayed behind at the trail head. She looked around and called louder, remembering that Emily Carr had said she was a little deaf. "Alex, are you there?" Some twigs cracked.

"Your brother probably went home," she said flatly, leaning heavily against a tree for a few minutes, mumbling something to herself.

Lee's body tightened. "I told you," she yelled, "Alex is my cousin. We don't live up there." Angry tears came to her eyes. "Believe me!"

"Yes, yes," Emily Carr started up again. "This has gone on long enough," she said. Turning to Lee, who had caught up with her, she asked, "Have you tried writing, or drawing or painting? You need to work with your anger in a different way. Write your stories down rather than trying to trick people."

Lee wished she had her easel. She'd paint LISTEN TO ME in huge black letters through red flames. As they puffed up the hill, Lee again tried to explain her problem. Emily Carr only mumbled, "Yes, you're good. Write it all down."

Lee wanted to scream, to cry, to kick the trees. The woman still didn't believe that this morning they'd been camped at the exact spot she was in now. Lee considered going back to the beach, to look for clues, to find tire marks. Then she realized Alex was there. She knew for sure that as long as the camp stayed empty, Alex would search the beach and the strange trailer. He was a good detective and he'd find something. Lee had to keep Emily Carr at the homestead as long as she could.

When they arrived at the clearing, Willard was sitting by the fire and stirring something in a pot.

"Your sister tells me your mother's hurt." Emily Carr walked to the pot and lifted the lid.

"My sister's in there with Ma." With his wooden spoon Willard pointed to the cabin. "Goat's milk. I'm boiling it for lunch." He petted one of the dogs.

"Your sister...oh!" Emily Carr looked at Lee. "I'll be," she mumbled. "I guess you're right." She scratched the back of her neck. "This *is* a different boy. So you don't belong here after all. Well, who *are* you then?"

Lee started explaining again, but Emily Carr waved

her arm. "Let's look at that leg first."

In the cabin Clare sat beside the bed, knitting. Her mother's eyes were closed. Emily Carr introduced herself before she told the girls to leave them. Clare insisted on staying, but Lee quickly went outside. She and Alex had told too many ghost stories in that room. It was spooky even if creepers no longer grew through the wall and the floor didn't creak with every step.

Walking to the fire, she asked, "Did you tear the old shacks down and build new cabins?"

"Old shacks? There weren't any. This land," Willard waved the spoon around, "we cleared when we got here." He went back to stirring the milk slowly.

"But the old shacks...the old apple trees...."

"Three years ago, when my pa 'nd Uncle John got here, there was nothing but forest."

Lee looked around, shaking her head. "We were here two weeks ago, Alex and Uncle Brooke and I. The shacks were old. That little one," Lee pointed to Uncle John's cabin, "had no floor. It was rotten– caved in. And...." Lee stopped. She looked from Willard to the cabins, back to Willard. "I don't get it," she said, scratching a mosquito bite so hard it started bleeding.

Willard moved the pot of milk onto a flat, hot rock and got up to collect branches for the fire. One of the dogs pulled at a stick. The boy threw it high and away into the bush where some dogs ran after it, tails wagging. Lee also started gathering an armful of branches.

When they returned to the fire, Willard stirred the

milk and said, "We built the big cabin when we got here two years ago. Pa 'nd Uncle John, they'd already cleared a small spot 'nd built the little cabin."

"No way." Lee threw her branches down by the fire pit.

Willard left to gather more wood.

Lee followed him again. "We were here," she said. "The shacks were old. Why is everybody lying? Where's my mother?" She grabbed Willard's arm.

He tried to shake loose, but dropped his branches instead. "I don't know," he shrugged. "You're the one that's lying 'nd acting strange. We've been here since 1934."

Lee let go of his arm. Maybe Alex had found some clues by now. Walking towards the trail, she stopped suddenly. 1934? She turned back to Willard. "Did you say 1934?"

Willard nodded.

"But that is..." Lee counted in her head. "That's more than sixty years ago."

Willard shook his head. "Two years ago," he said. "I know. Pa, he taught us to count. See?" Holding out his fingers, he tapped them as he said, "1935, 1936." He held up two fingers.

"That's ridiculous." Lee turned away in disgust. "Don't you even know it's 1996?"

"No. Pa says it's 1936. He doesn't lie." Willard glared at her.

Lee's stomach tightened. "Sure, Dad says he doesn't

lie either," she mumbled. She kicked a branch, picked it up and whacked it against a tree until it broke. "How do you know he's not lying." She stood in front of Willard, watching his face closely.

"He just doesn't." He kept gathering firewood.

"How can you be so sure?"

"I know Pa doesn't lie. He never has."

Lee picked up another stick, muttering, "He's wrong!" She broke the stick in two and threw the pieces away. One of the dogs ran after them.

Walking to the cabin, she looked at the new apple trees. They were in the same spot where the old, big gnarled ones had been a few weeks ago. How could they suddenly look so small? "It can't be," she said, going into the cabin.

She squinted in the semi-darkness. "What year is it?" she asked loudly. As her eyes got more used to the inside light, she saw three faces staring at her.

Emily Carr had wrapped a big bandage around the injured leg. "Well, 1936 of course. Here, hold your finger on this."

Lee put her finger on the knot and looked at Clare. The girl, who had turned back to rinsing something in the tub full of water, wore a strange dress, much like Emily Carr's. Both dresses came down almost to their calves. Maybe they wore dresses that looked like night gowns in 1936.

"This is stupid and I don't believe you!" Lee glared from one surprised face to the other. She pulled her finger away.

Emily Carr had finished tying the knot. She stood up slowly with a little groan and rubbed her hip. "I don't know where this girl came from, but she has no manners," she said, washing her hands at the tub and drying them on her dress. "She does make up good stories though. This woman needs rest. We'll leave her."

"I'll stay with her," Clare said, picking up her knitting.

As they walked out the door, Emily Carr patted Lee on the shoulder. She sat on a stump by the fire and said, "Oh, I'm bone weary. Now girl, tell us who you *really* are."

One more time Lee started to explain how they were camped at the beach this morning.

Emily Carr shook her head. "No, no, I'm the only one on that beach. I've been there several days. Now tell the truth."

At this Lee burst into tears. She tightened her fists. "I am telling the truth," she yelled. "We were at the beach, Alex and I. And our parents. But the trees are all...it's almost as if...."

It was as if she were in a different time. Could it really be sixty years ago? No, of course not. That was impossible. People didn't time travel. But these trees, and the cabins...this place *did* look as if.... If it was 1936, then in 1996 the apple trees would be old and gnarled. The cabins would be tumble-down shacks with creepers growing through holes in the walls. She looked at the woman and the boy by the fire.

"Where will you be sixty years from now?" she

asked. As soon as she'd said it, she wished she hadn't asked such a dumb question. How would they know? But then, Lee felt incredibly confused, as if someone had blindfolded her and spun her around and around, so she no longer knew what was forward and what was backward.

"So," she said slowly, realizing the fact as she said it, "if it's sixty years ago, then...well, then you're no longer alive...when I'm...." She frowned.

Emily Carr laughed. "I may be in poor health," she chuckled, "but I'm certainly not dead yet. Far from it. You do come up with interesting ideas though. If I could figure you out, maybe I could understand myself better." She rubbed her chin. "Yes, yes," she nodded, "a kindred spirit. So, do you paint, or write stories, or make up songs? It's easier for me to understand things when I put them down on paper– create."

"I write in my journal. Sometimes I paint," Lee said.

Emily Carr clapped her hands. "I knew it," she smiled.

"If it's 1936 I'm a long time from home. I'm in big trouble!" Lee felt her stomach lurch. Her legs were shaking so hard she had to sit down on a stump.

"These are troubled times," the painter said, nodding and cuddling Pout. "Are you an orphan? My mother died when I was young– only fourteen. I missed her terribly. My oldest sister had to look after me. I'm afraid I caused her no end of trouble."

Lee again told her story, but this time she included her fear about the time travel. "I know it doesn't make sense," she said, shaking her head.

Willard, putting more sticks on the fire, looked at her inquisitively.

"We must get to work, you and I," Emily Carr said. "Before you go back to wherever you came from, we must paint. I want to get to know you better."

She told Willard to let his mother rest and to give her healing teas. "Use this," she said, handing him a small can of leaves from her cloth bag. "And," she wagged her finger sternly, "come down and see me if you have any more trouble. I'll be around for a while." She didn't want the corn Willard offered, shaking her head and saying, "You need it more than I do."

"Come on girl," she said, smiling as she headed down the path. "We're going to paint." She started to hum a tune.

With her little hands the monkey had pulled pieces of bark off the tree to look for bugs. When she saw them coming she called, "Woo, woo." Emily Carr greeted her happily.

Stepping under the tarp that hung off the trailer, she gasped. "Someone was here," she cried. "Look at that." She flung the front tarp wide open. On a table and two old chairs lay brushes, cans of paints, manila paper, half-finished sketches and paintings. Boards lay on the ground beside cooking pans, buckets, tubs, dishes and groceries.

"Someone moved everything. It's all higgledy-piggledy." Emily Carr looked down the beach both ways. It was empty. She hurried into her trailer.

Did Alex find something? Lee wondered if she should help the woman clean up. Or maybe it was always this cluttered. Alex would have moved things back into their place. He was usually not destructive. Lee wanted to try to find Alex, but looking around, she didn't see any sign of him.

Walking back to the trail head, she quietly called his name. When there was no response, she called louder.

Perhaps he had gone farther along the beach, found the men and was spying on them. Lee walked around the rocky outcropping. As she neared the next cove, she crouched behind a big boulder and searched the area with her eyes. A long way off the fires still roared. Here nothing moved except the waves that rolled up onto the empty beach. She followed the edge of the trees, careful not to make any noise.

Suddenly she heard a twig snap. She stood motionless, hardly breathing. Her heart beat in her throat. Were the men nearby? She crawled past bushes, ready to flatten herself on the ground at any moment.

Lee waited several minutes, listening for voices. She could see the horses' brown bodies through the brush. One of the animals whinnied and snorted. The horses stood in the clearing, tied to ropes. Their harnesses had been removed. They both looked at her, then continued eating. One walked a few steps to a creek for a drink.

"Alex?" Lee called softly. No reply.

She followed the trail of horses' hoofprints to the beach. Something had been dragged from the forest to the high-tide line. Farther out a few fishing boats chugged along. Lee walked back to where the trail disappeared into the trees. The horses' harnesses, the sled with the anchor and the chains were stashed behind a tree.

"Alex," Lee called again, a little louder. She followed the big footprints to the high-tide mark. They disappeared at the water's edge. Lee searched up and down the cove for smaller shoe prints. Nothing.

Perhaps they took Alex. Maybe they had Mom and the others too.

She was here alone, Lee realized. Alone with Emily Carr. She wanted to paint. She wanted to forget about everybody, to brush all her frustrations onto a big piece of paper and disappear right into the painting.

When she arrived back at the camp, Emily Carr was just sitting down on her camp stool to paint. She faced the trees.

"Don't stare at my work," she growled. "There's yours." She pointed her brush at another board, brushes and paints lying on a stool closer to the water.

Lee didn't hesitate. All the anger, all the confusion, all the loneliness of the last few days rushed in a wave of emotion from her fingertips to the paper. Feelings flowed onto the paper: big swirling clouds, grey, white, huge blue waves crashing into the clouds, logs tumbling over each other. A man stood on a log, a suitcase in one hand, a framed picture in the other. A motorhome was partially visible in the water. The van lay crushed under a huge log, the headlights, like eyes, cracked.

She put her paint brush down. "There!" she sighed, feeling she'd said more with that one word than she had with all her yelling and door slamming.

"Yes, yes," Emily Carr beamed. She stood behind Lee and clapped. "It's alive. I see things in your work, hear them, taste them almost. They reach out to you: the trees, the water, the sky. Do you understand?"

Lee nodded. The anger that had burned inside her since Dad left was now in the painting instead. She felt free, even if she *was* lost.

"You're angry about the logging too– I see it," Emily Carr said. She brought her stool over and sat down beside Lee.

"It's my dad," Lee said. "I used to paint a lot at home. I had my own paints, brushes and an easel. I had this neat corner in my room where I worked on my art projects."

"Like a miniature studio," Emily Carr nodded. "My favorite studio was the loft of an old cow barn in Victoria. It was full of smells, noises, life. I loved it. I could really paint there."

Lee nodded. "I know how you feel. But a few weeks ago my dad got mad because Mom wouldn't give him any more money, so he sold all my painting supplies."

Lee talked about her dad's problem, his leaving, her anger. Emily Carr nodded from time to time, listening intently.

"I told him to quit drinking, but he never listened to me. I didn't know what to do or how to change things."

Emily Carr sighed. "My father sometimes did things I didn't like either, when I was small. And my oldest sister did too, after my mother died. It's not up to you to make things better. It's your father's own problem. No one else's. Painting is one way of making *yourself* feel better."

Lee realized that both here and at school Friday afternoon she had calmed herself down by putting her feelings into her art.

"My teacher likes you," she said. "We saw some of your paintings."

"Which ones?" Emily Carr leaned closer.

"*Forest Landscape,* I think," Lee said, trying to remember. "There were some big trees and some little ones in front of it. I love the way you made the swirly branches, like waves." She made circles in the air with her hands.

Emily Carr's eyebrows arched. "Who's your teacher?"

"Ms. Candle."

The painter shook her head. "I've never heard of her. I went to the Provincial Normal School last year to give a speech. And I gave sketching classes this summer. But...Ms. Candle?" She shook her head. "Did you say she had some of my paintings?"

"No, slides of them."

Emily Carr frowned. "I don't know about that. Maybe she saw some of my work at an art exhibit." She beamed suddenly. "People come and see my paintings, you know. But how could she have seen something I haven't finished?" She stood up and walked toward her own board.

Lee saw the sketch the painter was working on. "It's like the other one," she said. "The one you called *Rebirth*. I remember it clearly. I liked it a lot. I was so mad on Friday, I wanted to walk right into those trees, disappear and be reborn too. I love the bright colours."

Emily Carr shook her head. "I can't believe your teacher showed you my work, but you are delightful." She took Lee's painting off the board. "I'll get you another sheet of paper. You're not finished this story. And tell me about these strange things you've painted. What's this vehicle that looks like a truck?"

"I don't have time. I have to find Mom and Alex and Uncle Brooke." Lee started toward the other cove again. She stopped a few feet away and turned. "That family is keeping a secret," she said.

"Of course. They live up there illegally. They're cutting trees without a permit."

"Why?" Lee looked at the trail head.

"They're poor. They're trying to make a living. They probably sell that wood to carvers in Victoria."

"They're not allowed to be here?"

"No. They didn't buy the land. They're hoping they

won't be found." Emily Carr put another sheet on Lee's board. "Here," she said. "Paint what you see."

Lee thought Alex could wait a few minutes longer. She had to paint, to paint the twins' story: living under a wagon, their Ma under a pile of garbage, rats scurrying around her, nibbling at half-rotten bits of food.

"I hope nobody finds them," she said, moving toward the easel.

Emily Carr nodded. "I won't tell. It's better than being homeless. Better than what those other 'real' loggers are doing." She pointed to the beach with the fires and shook her head. "They kill everything. Shrubs, creatures, everything. But they have permits. It's crazy, unfair."

"Mom gets really mad about clear-cut logging too. She went to a protest once and got chained to a tree."

"To become one with the tree spirit?" Emily Carr smiled dreamily.

"No, to stop loggers from cutting it down. She lay in front of a big truck once too. The police came." Lee frowned. "It was kind of scary."

The painter nodded. "She loves the trees, like I do. She's brave."

"Yes." Lee nodded. "I like these trees too. They look so strong with all the growth up there and on the ground, like a jungle."

"They're very old and wise– they are our guardians." Emily Carr turned to look at the fires again. "That's why I worry about the destruction, killing all these spirits. That's what scares me. The land will never be the same again."

Lee nodded. "When you look out now it's much greener because the trees are so thick, like the swirly strokes in your paintings. When you're at Lookout Point where I live...I mean, in my time...it's so...well, so thin, so scrawny, compared to now. I wish they would leave all these trees here." She swept her arm around to the forest behind her. "When I get back home I'm going to help Mom fight to keep it this way."

Suddenly she had an idea– maybe Alex went up to Lookout Point, to scan the whole stretch of beach.

"I've got to go," she said abruptly, getting up from her easel and stool. She headed for the trail.

Near the first bend in the path she glanced over her shoulder. Emily Carr stood on the beach with her dogs and her monkey, looking at her. She held Lee's painting in her hand.

As Lee turned back to the path, she felt her foot catch on a root and heard a dull *thud* as her head hit a rock.

Voices echoed in the darkness, in her head, as if they were calling from across the water at night. The sounds came closer. Familiar voices surrounded her.

Slowly Lee opened her eyes. "Alex, you're back. You found them."

Mom, Uncle Brooke and Pat were bent over her. They looked worried. Uncle Brooke was holding her wrist and looking at his watch.

"What do you mean?" Alex asked.

"Don't talk," Uncle Brooke said. "You hit your head. You may have a concussion."

"Honey, are you all right?" Mom's face came closer.

Lee looked at them. "But, you were gone. I was...."

Uncle Brooke interrupted her. "You were unconscious for a while." His hands carefully examined her head. "Your head's not bleeding, but you'll have a big, sore lump," he said finally.

"I know," Lee whispered.

"Stay quiet," Mom said. "Can she walk, Brooke?"

"We'll carry her. Sit up slowly." Her uncle and her mother hooked hands, eased Lee onto them and lifted her up.

Lee put her arms around their necks. "I'm so glad to see you," she whispered. She rested her head on Mom's shoulder.

Her mother smiled. "You'll be fine."

Lee looked down at the beach. Emily Carr, her monkey, her dogs, the camp stools and the boards were gone. When they turned off the trail, Lee saw that the elephant was no longer there. The whole, huge contraption had disappeared, tarps and all. Their own camping vehicles stood where they were before. The fire pit no longer had bricks holding a grill and a kettle. The tubes lay by the slide.

When they arrived back at the campsite, Mom took some pillows from the van. Uncle Brooke pulled his chair into the shade of the blue awning. "You relax on this," he said. "I'll get an ice pack for your head. You need plenty of rest today."

"Alex, you remember Emily Carr, don't you?" Lee felt confused. It must be the headache and the throbbing lump.

"Emily Carr? Who's that?" Alex put more sunscreen on his nose.

Lee couldn't believe her ears. "You were there," she said sharply.

"I came back here, to get Dad." Alex made a face.

"Man, were you ever conked out."

Lee looked at the trees around her. They were no longer huge, but instead the small regular trees and shrubs she had always remembered. While Uncle Brooke poured tall glasses of cranberry juice, she told her story. She concluded, "But if it never happened, then how would I know so much about Emily Carr, and Woo and the homestead family?"

Mom patted Lee's hand. "You learned about Emily Carr on Friday at school. Remember? You told me."

"Not *that* much." Lee sat up, her arm tired from holding the ice pack. "I met her," she insisted.

"Sleep a while," Mom suggested.

"No sleeping right after that fall," Uncle Brooke said. "First we make sure she doesn't have a concussion."

Her uncle stared at Lee and scratched his head under his cap. "Strange," he said after a few seconds of silence. "I just read something about people who think they may have time travelled, many of them while they were unconscious. Where's that magazine?" He got up and disappeared into the motorhome.

Alex got his comics out. Pat read a book.

Lee looked at her arms and legs. At the homestead she had scratched till the mosquito bites bled. Now her skin was smooth, with no bites anywhere and none on Alex's arms and legs either.

"How's your head?" Mom took the ice pack and looked at the lump.

"Getting better." Lee leaned back.

"I don't have that article here." Uncle Brooke sat down on the other side of Lee. "Maybe in your former life you lived at that homestead. Although," he gave Lee a puzzled look, "Alex wouldn't have been there. And you wouldn't have worried about finding us. Hmmmm." He shook his head slowly.

"Maybe the injury is more serious than we thought." Mom frowned.

He kept shaking his head, an inquisitive look on his face. "I don't know enough about time travel to guess at the side effects."

Lee rubbed her arms. "I had so many mosquito bites just a few hours ago, but now...." She shrugged her shoulders.

"Oh, in those days, yes, I don't doubt it," Her uncle said. "And no insect repellent, I bet."

Lee shook her head. "Not at the homestead. I wonder. My painting...Emily Carr kept it." She sat up and looked around again at the trees and shrubs. "I know I met her."

Uncle Brooke smiled. "I believe you. Maybe you met, or," he nodded, a slight twinkle in his eyes, "maybe you *were* Emily Carr."

Lee frowned. "Well," she said, feeling even more confused.

He laughed and said, "At least you're okay now. Say, you might like to read some of her autobiographies, you know, books she wrote about herself. There's one called *The Book of Small,* about her childhood. There are others too. I'm sure they're in the library." He took a tiny bite from a piece of carrot cake and chewed slowly and deliberately.

"Are you sure Alex was there?" he said, when he finished the bite. "Could it have been a different boy? The homestead boy?"

"It was Alex, but I wonder, what *did* happen to Willard and Clare and their family?"

Uncle Brooke asked, "Do you know their last name? We can look in the archives." When Lee shook her head he said, "We'll check it out anyway. You never know what we'll dig up."

Lee began to get excited. "I wonder if they went to school. I hope they never got caught for illegal logging."

"Probably not," Uncle Brooke said. "Times were tough then, during the Depression. They probably moved when there were more jobs again, after the Second World War."

Everyone relaxed in the shade. Lee felt the ice pack slipping.

Uncle Brooke wiped his long fingers on a napkin, took the ice pack and put it on the table. "Do you have paints?" he asked.

"I used to," Lee said, stretching. "But at Dad's garage sale...."

"Oh yes," was all her uncle said.

"Can people really time travel?" Lee asked, feeling a little silly.

"Scientists are starting to study it more. There are important questions about the brain they can't answer yet." Her uncle put his hands together, fingertips touching. He nodded and said, "Who knows what's possible?"

"I met those people, and their stories were hard to believe too, but I listened. Could it really be true, the story Clare told me about millions of grasshoppers? The dust storms, the hard times?"

"Yes, those things happened on the prairies around 1931 or 1932, I think."

"I drank the water from the creek," Lee said. When she saw her uncle frown, she added, "Clare and Willard drink it all the time."

"Back then, I guess it wasn't so polluted," he said, reaching for his glass of juice and passing Lee hers.

"I liked the trees that were here then. They looked so strong, so huge, giants. Let's go up there." Lee sat up and pointed to the peak.

"Next weekend. Today you take it easy." Her uncle refilled their glasses.

Lee decided she'd write this whole adventure in her journal as soon as she got home. Just like Emily Carr had said, writing was a way she could understand what happened in her life, make it seem more real. Then she'd have it forever. She couldn't wait until Friday's art lesson so that she could paint the story of this day. She wanted to learn more about Emily Carr and to imagine what other adventures she might have under Emily's sky.